The Dog Prince

An original fairy tale by Lauren Mills

illustrated by Lauren Mills
& Dennis Nolan

LITTLE, BROWN AND COMPANY
BOSTON   NEW YORK   LONDON

First Edition

Library of Congress Cataloging-in-Publication Data

Mills, Lauren A.
    The dog prince / by Lauren Mills ; illustrated by Lauren Mills and Dennis
Nolan — 1st ed.
        p. cm.
    Summary: While hunting the beast known as the chimera, an arrogant prince
is turned into a dog and must learn humility from a gentle goat-girl.
    ISBN 0-316-57417-1
    [1. Behavior — Fiction. 2. Magic — Fiction. 3. Princes — Fiction. 4. Dogs —
Fiction. 5. Monsters — Fiction.] I. Nolan, Dennis, ill. II. Title.

PZ7.M63979 Do 1996
[E] — dc20   95-005302

10 9 8 7 6 5 4 3 2 1

TWP

Printed in Singapore

The illustrations for this book were done in watercolor with pencil on D'Arches watercolor paper.
The text was set in Minister Light, and the display type is Mantegna.

Author's Note

The chimera (pronounced kye-MEER-uh) is a monster from Greek mythology, with the head of a lion, the body of a she-goat, and the tail of a serpent. The word *chimera* also refers to an illusion, especially a seemingly unrealizable dream.

This book is dedicated to all those who are willing to risk everything for their dream.... And also—

To our editor,

Maria Modugno,

who never once doubted.

The prince was bored by his devoted people, bored by his elegant castle, bored by his perfect garden, his fancy meals, his royal clothes. He was bored by his life as a prince.

One hundred young ladies in their finest dresses waited eagerly at the castle gate for the prince to rouse and take his morning stroll. They had stood for hours, hoping to catch just a glimpse of their handsome prince, and now their toes, cramped in tiny shoes, began to blister.

From out of the forest appeared a wizened little woman. She shuffled up to the discouraged girls. "Now, what seems to be the problem?" she asked.

"The prince refuses to get out of bed!" lamented one girl. "This is the cruelest thing he has ever done."

The old woman chuckled, shook her head, and walked on by. As she passed the gardener, she called out, "Congratulations, sir."

The gardener turned around. "What have I done, old Nana?"

"Why, don't you know? You have grown the finest roses in all the world!"

The gardener looked at his roses and mopped his forehead. "If only the prince saw with your eyes."

"Ha!" cackled the old woman. "When one has everything, one notices nothing. That's what comes of being spoiled."

"Ah, he is spoiled — that he is," agreed the gardener. "There is nothing left for him to *want*. He says he won't even go hunting anymore, because all that remains in the forest now are rabbits, and what sort of challenge is that?"

"'Tis a challenge for the poor rabbits!" said the old woman with a laugh. "Well, he'll soon cause himself a challenge, anyhow," she continued, "and if he's of any noble blood, he ought to fix what he has done!"

"What are you saying, old Nana?" the gardener asked.

"I mean that it will be his own fault when the chimera prowls about the farmlands looking for something to eat. The prince has left nothing else for her in the wild. He needs to deal with the chimera *now* before we start to lose all our sheep and goats!"

"Chimera? I've never heard of such a beast," said the gardener doubtfully.

"Perhaps you've been tending these roses too long, good fellow. The chimera is the lion-headed she-goat with the tail of a serpent. Her fiery eyes alone could bring an entire army of knights down on their knees. She'll be the death of us all if…" The old woman squinted up at the prince's window and huffed. "Well, good day, sir," she said, and shuffled away.

"Hmmm. A chimera," said the gardener to himself. "Yes, I believe the prince might rouse for that sort of challenge."

No sooner had the prince heard news of the chimera than he was out of bed, ordering horses, huntsmen, and a coach to prepare to hunt the fabled beast.

"The prince is coming! The prince is coming!" The cry spread through the town like a runaway river, so that when the prince's coach reached the square, the streets were filled with people.

There was not a maiden whose cheeks did not turn pink upon seeing the handsome prince. "How they stare," snapped the prince. "Disgusting! Don't they have anything better to do? Driver, clear the way," he demanded.

"Away with you!" shouted the driver, and he cracked his whip in the air. The horses snorted and reared, sending the crowd away screaming.

"That's better," said the prince as the coach sped down the street.

The hunting party began their climb up the narrow mountain road, but they soon came upon a goat girl herding her goats. With high hedges on either side, there was no room for a coach to pass.

"Bother!" shouted the prince. "We will never get there!"

The goat girl spun around, and as soon as her eyes fell upon the handsome prince, her mouth dropped open.

"Well, what are *you* gaping at?" demanded the prince.

Her cheeks flushed. "Forgive me, my lord," she answered. "I shall hurry my goats as fast as I can." She then gave a grand curtsy more befitting a princess than a poor goat girl in a tattered dress.

The huntsmen bent over with laughter. "Goat girl, where did *you* learn such a curtsy?" one called out. "Is your mother a queen?"

The goat girl pretended not to hear. She darted after her goats, but the huntsmen continued to taunt her. When she stumbled on a sharp stone, they noticed her feet had nothing to cover them but dirt. "My, what royal shoes you wear, goat girl."

At this, the goat girl grew angry and slowed to a walk.

"Oh, bother," said the prince again. "Goat girl, will you kindly move a little faster?"

But the goat girl surprised them all and glared at the prince. "No, I will NOT," she said boldly. Tears welled in her eyes, but she held her gaze.

The prince now felt truly sorry for what they had done but was too proud to say so, especially in front of his huntsmen.

"What impertinence! Shall I arrest her, my lord?" asked the driver.

"No," answered the prince, looking into her eyes — *Eyes that are like a chimera's,* he thought.

The goat girl turned and slowly walked on.

When they reached a fork in the road, the goat girl continued up the mountain path, but the prince impatiently chose the road that led into the dark forest.

Before long, the hunting party came to a narrow bridge. Old Nana was hanging out her laundry to dry across the bridge railings.

The prince huffed. "We're in a hurry, woman. Remove your rags at once or we'll trample them."

The old woman slowly picked up her laundry piece by piece, carefully smoothing out each garment before placing it in her basket.

"Faster!" commanded the prince.

"Perhaps if you would care to help old Nana, it would take less time," the little woman answered calmly.

The prince lost all patience. "Crone, I am the *prince*! I have no time for this!" He took the whip himself and cracked it over the horses' backs, and the coach rushed across the bridge, trampling all of the old woman's laundry.

Now, it so happened that the old woman was a faery, and she chanted a curse after them: *"Hunters to crows and prince to hound!"*

Instantly the huntsmen turned to crows. They awkwardly flapped their wings. *"Caw, caw, caw!"* they screeched, and flew off. At the same time, the once-handsome prince turned into a big, baggy-eyed bloodhound. He circled around the old faery and growled at her.

Tossing her head with a laugh, the faery said, "Be off, before I turn you into a frog and SQUASH you!"

The dog prince tucked his tail between his legs and bounded away. He never knew how he made it down that rocky mountain road, his legs were shaking so. When he reached the town, he was out of breath and panting from thirst. He headed straight for the town fountain, but crowding around it were all the townspeople, still chatting about the prince.

"Without a doubt, he looked at me from the corner of his eye as he passed by," said one girl, pinning her hair in place.

"Oh, no, it was not you he was looking at," said another. "It was me! I was standing right behind you...." And the conversation went on like this while their fine dresses swished round and round. Nowhere was there room for a thirsty hound dog to slip in for a drink from the fountain. However, the dog prince, encouraged by their fond talk of him, nosed in closer. As soon as the young ladies noticed him, they gasped. "Disgusting! Look how he slobbers! Shoo, dog, shoo!" And they poked him with the tips of their parasols.

The prince might have cried if he'd had tears to cry, but a dog can only whine or slink away. The dog prince did both.

With nowhere to go but home, the prince returned to his castle, where he sniffed at the crack in the kitchen doorway and smelled a delicious roast cooking. He barked and waited with his mouth watering, but to his dismay, the cook, whom he once knew to be kind and generous, chased him away!

Over on the west wall, the prince heard *"Caw! Caw!"* and he knew at once that it was his huntsmen calling. *"Aa-roof! Aa-roof!"* he barked in reply. *"Caw! Caw!"* they answered back. This continued for some time until the gardener could stand it no longer and began to throw rocks at the hound.

"Be gone!" yelled the gardener. "You don't belong here!"

So the poor prince loped away from the castle that was once his home. He foraged through garbage heaps for a few scraps of supper, and afterward he found a thicket off the mountain road where he could lie down for the night. But sleep? He did not. Instead, he howled at the moon and thought, *Oh, how bitter and harsh my life has become.*

The dog prince was still whimpering the next morning when he heard a kind voice say, "Poor dog, you must be lost."

He looked up and saw the same goat girl he had been rude to only the day before. But what fortune! What glory! She was smiling at him now! He was so pleased that his tail wagged back and forth with such a force that it whipped his sides.

"I'm Eliza," said the goat girl, holding out a piece of cheese for him. The prince rushed to eat it.

"Not so fast!" said Eliza, but he jumped up anyway and knocked her over. Eliza's goats promptly butted him.

"You see? You're too impatient," said Eliza. "You must learn some manners. Now, sit."

The dog prince whined and circled and dodged the goats, thinking all the while, *I'm a prince, I'm a prince,* until at last he decided it was no use. He sat.

"Good dog! That's better." Eliza handed him the cheese, which tasted more delicious to him than anything he remembered. She patted him gently. Ah, he could smell the sweet fragrance of pine and wildflowers in her hair. Then he looked into her eyes and saw they were not angry, as they had been the day before, but caring. *Nothing could be more beautiful,* he thought with a sigh. He tucked his nose into her arm, feeling glad that she did not recognize him for who he truly was.

Eliza continued up the mountain road with her goats. The dog prince followed behind — but far enough behind so that the goats would not butt him.

Eliza turned and smiled. "Yesterday a prince followed me, and today, you! I think I shall call you Prince, though I like you much better than that rude man."

The prince whined a little but continued to follow her.

When Eliza brought Prince home, her father told her, "Very well, you may keep him, but he sleeps outside."

From that day on, Prince followed Eliza everywhere while she continued to teach him patience and manners and how to herd the goats. Eliza loved his company, and even the goats didn't seem to mind him, as long as he behaved. Prince was beginning to feel that life as Eliza's dog wasn't all that bad. When he sat beneath the beech tree with Eliza, there was nothing more he could want. The only times he wished he were not her dog were when she spoke of her dreams. Then, how he wished he were human and could just talk to her!

There were even some small challenges that Prince had never dreamt of enjoying. One of them was fetching sticks for Eliza. *If only I could do more for her,* he thought one day as his nose was in the hedgerow searching for a lost stick. Suddenly he heard a gunshot and raced back down the road. The goats were crying and darting every which way while Eliza was trying to calm them. Prince recognized the men in a royal coach. They were his officials, and they were searching for *him,* at last! He could have licked their faces — until he heard the driver yell, "I'll say it one more time, filthy lass! Get your goats out of our way or I'll crack this whip over all of you."

Prince's tail stopped wagging, and the hair on the back of his neck stood up. *How dare they treat Eliza like that!* He circled the horses and snarled. The driver tried to whip him but struck his own horses instead.

"Now look what your dog has done!" the driver cried out. "He's spooked our horses!" The coach swayed dangerously as the horses reared. "Call him off before there's an accident!"

"Back your horses down the hill," said Eliza calmly, "and then I will call my dog."

Prince bared his sharp teeth. The driver had no choice. He backed his horses down the hill.

Prince trotted beside Eliza like her proud knight. Patting his head, Eliza said, "You are much more noble than any man. I'll *never* marry. . . . And I don't care what has happened to that awful prince!"

No longer feeling proud, Prince lowered his head. When they reached the next fork, Eliza took the road that led into the woods.

"Come, Prince. I need you to help Nana," Eliza called. But Prince remembered that dark road . . . and Nana. He whined and paced back and forth, refusing to enter those woods, until finally Eliza grew impatient and commanded him to do so.

When the old faery woman saw who Eliza had brought with her, she chuckled.

"Nana, he's really quite smart and has learned to be so well mannered," Eliza told her.

"Pff! When a dog is hungry, he'll do anything," responded Nana.

A low growl came from Prince.

"Prince!" exclaimed Eliza in horror. "Shame on you! Come over here and lie down."

"Once a dog, always a dog," muttered the old faery woman, looking straight at Prince, but then she added, "unless, of course, he proves himself worthy of his name."

Prince watched them carry the laundry in small sacks over the bridge. Then, gently taking a sack in his mouth, he did the same.

"Very good," said the faery woman, nodding. "You've decided to be useful after all." Then, with a pat on his head, she whispered to him, "'Tis love that has taught you to care, eh, pup?"

As they returned home, Prince would not play fetch. All he wanted was to walk by Eliza's side. He wanted to tell her that he knew at last what he had been hunting for in his life. It was not the chimera. It was Eliza. She had opened his heart, but what good was an open heart to him now, locked inside a dog's body?

This was the sorrowful question that kept the dog prince awake all night. How he wished for the darkness to end, but it wore on and on until it came to its final hour, the hour when anything might happen, for better or for worse. It was at that hour that Prince met his challenge.

It mysteriously appeared, a shimmering form at first, twisting and turning between the rocks. Then there was no mistaking it . . . the *chimera!*

The lion-headed beast went directly to where the goats slept.

Prince growled. Boldly and slowly, the chimera faced him with fierce, glowing eyes, and Prince knew at once what those eyes told him: *"I dare you to come to me."*

Prince gulped. The beast was monstrous. With no trouble she could tear out his heart, but he could not let her take Eliza's flock. *Let her take my heart, then,* Prince thought. *Yes, for Eliza, I will give my heart.*

Eliza and her father woke to the terrifying sounds of hissing and growling. They ran outside and saw Prince desperately fighting the chimera.

Eliza's father held her back as she watched helplessly. The chimera tossed Prince into the air with her huge horns, then descended upon his chest. All seemed lost for Prince, but with a wild shout, Eliza ran recklessly from her father and smacked the back of the chimera with a broom!

The beast turned, baring her horrible fangs. Eliza screamed and began to run but knew she could not make it back to the house safely. Yet, to her amazement, she was not attacked. Prince had roused when he heard Eliza scream, and with his last bit of strength, which love had granted him, he clamped his jaws around the chimera and broke the beast's mighty neck.

The chimera lay still. Prince stumbled toward Eliza, then fell.

"I'll fetch some bandages," said Eliza's father, running into the house. Eliza laid her head on Prince's chest. He was barely breathing.

"No, Prince, no. You can't die. You're my best friend." Eliza cried as if her heart would break. "Prince, don't leave me. I love you." His baggy eyelids slowly folded shut, and Eliza bent down and kissed him.

All at once she jumped back, for it was no longer her dog lying there, and in the dusky light she saw well enough that it was the handsome prince!

"YOU!" she gasped. "What are *you* doing here? What happened to my dog?"

"You've changed me, Eliza," whispered the prince with a smile. "You've broken the spell."

Eliza shook her head doubtfully. "And you . . . are not hurt?" she finally asked, carefully touching his chest.

He took her hand. "No, not anymore. . . . That is, unless you do not want me, for then my heart shall surely break. But I've changed. I'm not the same person I was, and it's all because of you. Marry me, Eliza, if you could love me as a prince. If not, then I shall wish to be your dog again."

Then Eliza's eyes met his, and she recognized him for who he truly was. She nodded yes. The prince pulled her close and was kissing her just as Eliza's father came running out with the bandages.

Eliza looked up at her father. "Oh, we won't be needing those, Papa. He's better now," she said, leading the prince inside. Eliza's father stood outside scratching his chin for the longest time.

As the sun rose over the mountain, the old faery woman came riding up in the prince's hunting coach. Eliza and the prince ran out to greet her.

"Never once did I doubt, never once," cried the little woman, embracing them both. Then she handed them her laundry baskets. To their amazement, one after another was filled with the finest faery-made linens, laces, silk dresses, and yes, even shoes . . . all for the bride-to-be.

"Oh, Nana, I knew you were good, but I never knew you were a *faery!*" exclaimed Eliza.

"I knew she was a faery," said the prince, "but I didn't know she was *good!*"

"Pff, pff, enough silly talk. Now, Eliza, let's go inside and dress you up a bit," said old Nana.

When the prince saw Eliza looking so lovely, he could not find words to speak. All he could do was stare.

"Would you care to take the chimera back with you?" Eliza's father asked him.

"No," murmured the prince, without taking his eyes off Eliza. "Your daughter is all I want."

And with that, the chimera melted into a white swirling mist, growing smaller and smaller until at last it was merely a rabbit, which scampered away to hide itself beneath the earth.

Eliza and the prince rode off to the castle, with the herd of goats trailing behind them, followed by Eliza's proud father and old Nana. Everyone greeted the young couple warmly, including the huntsmen, who had changed back from crows to their former selves when the prince had been transformed. However, they were a little worse for having dropped from the trees.

And the prince, still a trifle impatient, held the wedding that very night, but Eliza and the prince chose *not* to live at the castle. Instead they lived high in the mountains, where they raised plenty of goats, some fine children, and a faithful dog.